and the
GINORMOUS GIANT

Rose Impey · Katharine McEwen

ORCHARD

Cast of Characters

Sir Lance-a-Little

Harold the Horse

Princess Plum

Huffalot the Dragon

The Ginormous Giant

At long last, Sir Lance-a-Little
and his No. 1 enemy, Huffalot
the dragon, were face to face and
about to do battle.

Huffalot really was enormous, with a long, scaly tail and lots of big, pointy teeth … not to mention his hot, fiery breath.

But Sir Lance-a-Little wasn't afraid! He had his sharp sword and his shiny shield … and he was, after all, the bravest little knight in the whole of Notalot.

Sir Lance-a-Little was rather disappointed that, for once, his annoying little cousin wasn't there. He would have liked Princess Plum to see him finally defeat his enemy.

"Ready when you are," Sir Lance-

a-Little told the dragon.

He raised his lance and prepared

to charge.

Suddenly, he heard

a familiar voice

calling ...

Help! Somebody ... h-e-l-l-l-p!

9

Sir Lance-a-Little and Huffalot
felt the ground beneath them
shudder. *Boom! Boom! Boom!*
At that moment, Princess Plum
came racing out of the woods,
waving her arms in the air.

Above the treetops was the largest head they'd ever seen. Even larger than the dragon's!
It was the head of an absolutely Ginormous Giant.

"Help!" cried Princess Plum. "He's going to eat me!"

Everyone turned and raced for the castle. They crossed the moat … closed the gates … and hauled up the drawbridge. Just in time.

The giant stood before the
castle walls and, in the most
ginormous voice, bellowed,
"Fee-fi-fo-fum,
You'll soon be in
my tum!"

"We'll see about that," huffed
Huffalot.

"Too right," said Sir Lance-a-Little.
The two sworn enemies agreed to
postpone their battle, while they
faced this new enemy.

Sir Lance-a-Little was ready to fight the giant on his own. After all, the dragon was pretty huge and he wasn't afraid of *him*.

"Leave this to me," he said bravely.

He stood on the castle battlements, throwing spears at the giant.

In no time, the Ginormous Giant looked like a ginormous porcupine.

But the giant hardly seemed to
notice. He plucked the spears out
and threw them aside as if they
were no more than splinters.

Next the dragon decided to take over.

"Leave this to me," he said

pompously.

Huffalot puffed up his chest and

huffed out huge flames, setting the

giant's feet on fire.

But again the giant hardly seemed
to notice.

He simply paddled in the moat to
cool them off. Unfortunately, this
caused a huge tidal wave of water.

It washed over the castle walls
and soaked everyone inside.
Sir Lance-a-Little and the dragon
glared at one another.

Princess Plum was cross with them both, but most cross with the giant. "You big bully," she shouted. "Pick on someone your own size!"

This made the giant very cross himself. He began to pull huge stones from the castle walls with his bare hands. Quite soon he would be able to step over the walls and grab them.

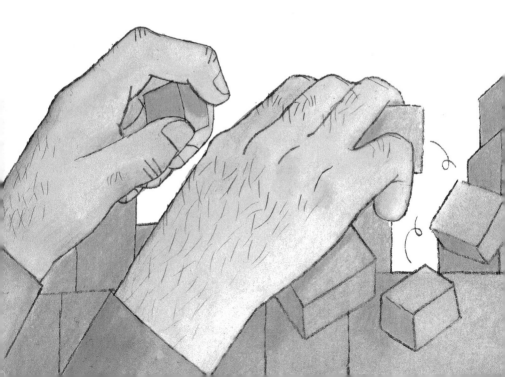

They all ran as fast as they could

to escape.

"If only we had some boiling oil!"

said Sir Lance-a-Little.

"There may be some soup,"

suggested Princess Plum. But

how to heat it up ...?

There was no time to make a
fire. By now the giant was almost
inside the castle.

"Who needs a fire," said Huffalot,
"when you've got me?"

The dragon used the last of his flames to heat up a big cauldron of soup and poured it ...

... all over the giant's head!

The giant couldn't see a thing. He lumbered around, bumping into trees and knocking them over. He roared so loudly that the whole castle shook.

When he found the path, the
Ginormous Giant headed off,
still bellowing with rage, until he
finally disappeared …
Boom! Boom! Boom!

Sir Lance-a-Little and
Princess Plum
cheered.

Hurrah!

They nervously
shook Huffalot's
enormous paw.

"What about your fight?"
Princess Plum asked.
But the two old enemies
were far too busy patting each
other on the back.
"Jolly good spear-throwing,"
said the dragon.

Excellent flames!

Of course, this didn't mean they wouldn't soon be sworn enemies again. A new challenge would surely be on its way, tomorrow ... or the next day.

"Definitely," said Huffalot, rattling his long, green, scaly tail. "Depend on it," said Sir Lance-a-Little, waving his sword.

THE END

Join the bravest knight in Notalot for all his adventures!

Written by Rose Impey • Illustrated by Katharine McEwen

Orchard Books are available from all good bookshops, or can be ordered from our website:
www.orchardbooks.co.uk
or telephone 01235 400400, or fax 01235 400454.

Prices and availability are subject to change.